First experiences
Staying the night

W
FRANKLIN WATTS
NEW YORK · LONDON · SYDNEY

Mum and Dad waved goodbye.

"Be a good boy Sam, and we'll see you in the morning."

"Tea time," smiled Gran.
Sam climbed up onto the chair.
"I can't see," he wailed.

Gran put him on the high stool.
"I don't like it here," said Sam.
"It's too wobbly."

Sam made a big mess on the floor but Gran didn't mind.

She made a little
picnic on the rug and they both
sat on cushions.

"Let's get you cleaned up,"
said Gran. The bubbles in the bath
smelt lovely and flowery.

Sam had a long splashy time making bubble hats and beards for himself and Gran.

Sam lay in bed. The room did not look right. It wasn't the same as his bedroom.

He wanted his Mum and Dad.

"I don't like it in here," Sam cried.
"You can sleep in my bed,
if you like," said Gran.

Gran's bed was as big as a bus and very soft. Sam bounced. Teddy bounced too.

Gran closed the door. A dark shape appeared in the shadows. "Aahh!" screamed Sam.

"There's a monster here," Sam sobbed.
"No, silly," said Gran, "it's
my dressing gown."

Gran gave Sam a big cuddle by the fire. He put his head on Gran's shoulder and watched the flames.

"Goodnight Gran," Sam whispered.
But Gran was already fast asleep.

These are the things
Sam packed for his
night away from home.
What would you take
with you?

Sharing books with your child

Early Worms are a range of books for you to share with your child. Together you can look at the pictures and talk about the subject or story. Listening, looking and talking are the first vital stages in children's reading development, and lay the early foundation for good reading habits.

Talking about the pictures is the first step in involving children in the pages of a book, especially if the subject or story can be related to their own familiar world. When children can relate the matter in the book to their own experience, this can be used as a starting point for introducing new knowledge, whether it is counting, getting to know colours or finding out how other people live.

Gradually children will develop their listening and concentration skills as well as a sense of what a book is. Soon they will learn how a book works: that you turn the pages from right to left, and read the story from left to right on a double page. They start to realize that the black marks on the page have a meaning and that they relate to the pictures. Once children have grasped these basic essentials they will develop strategies for "decoding" the text such as matching words and pictures, and recognising the rhythm of the language in order to predict what comes next. Soon they will start to take over the role of an independent reader, handling and looking at books even if they can't yet read the words.

Most important of all, children should realize that books are a source of pleasure. This stems from your reading sessions which are times of mutual enjoyment and shared experience. It is then that children find the key to becoming real readers.

First published in 1997
This edition published 2000
by Franklin Watts
96 Leonard Street,
London EC2A 4XD

Franklin Watts Australia
14 Mars Road
Lane Cove
NSW 2066

Text copyright
© Lisa Bruce 1997, 2000
Illustrations copyright
© Susie Jenkin-Pearce 1997, 2000

Series editor: Paula Borton
Art director: Robert Walster

Photography Steve Shott
With thanks to Ben Ridley-Johnson

A CIP catalogue record for this
book is available from the British
Library.

ISBN 0 7496 2775 1 (hbk)
ISBN 0 7496 3490 1 (pbk)

Dewey Classification 649

Printed in Belgium

Consultant advice: Sue Robson and Alison Kelly, Senior Lecturers in Education,
Faculty of Education, Early Childhood Centre, Roehampton Institute, London.

Paperback titles in this series:

Pets	Weather	Who are you?	Time	First Experiences
Guinea Pig	Windy day	In the Sea	Morning time	New shoes
0 7496 3498 7	0 7496 3497 9	0 7496 3510 X	0 7496 3487 1	0 7496 3492 8
Kitten	Snowy day	In the Polar Lands	Play time	A party
0 7496 3499 5	0 7496 3495 2	0 7496 3511 8	0 7496 3488 X	0 7496 3491 X
Puppy	Sunny day	On the Farm	Shopping time	Staying the night
0 7496 3500 2	0 7496 3496 0	0 7496 3512 6	0 7496 3489 8	0 7496 3490 1
Rabbit	Rainy day	In the Rainforest	Bed time	Big bed
0 7496 3501 0	0 7496 3494 4	0 7496 3513 4	0 7496 3486 3	0 7496 3493 6